W9-BDN-643

PEANUTS®

A Valentine for LINUS!

By Charles M. Schulz

Adapted by Jason Cooper
Illustrated by Scott Jeralds

SIMON SPOTLIGHT
An imprint of Simon & Schuster Children's Publishing Division
New York London Toronto Sydney New Delhi
1230 Avenue of the Americas, New York, New York 10020
This Simon Spotlight paperback edition December 2018
© 2018 Peanuts Worldwide LLC
For information about special discounts for bulk purchases, please contact Simon & Schuster
Special Sales at 1-866-506-1949 or business@simonandschuster.com.
Manufactured in the United States of America 1018 LAK
2 4 6 8 10 9 7 5 3 1
ISBN 978-1-5344-2043-4
ISBN 978-1-5344-2044-1 (eBook)

Valentine's Day was just around the corner, and Linus wanted to give a valentine to someone very special: his friend Lydia. She sat right behind him at school, and Linus found her quite interesting. And, sometimes, a bit frustrating . . .

"Lydia, how would you feel if I gave you a valentine?" Linus asked.

"I don't know," Lydia said. "Aren't you a little old for me?"

Linus shook his head. "I'm only two months older than you!" he said.

"Yes, but the months have not been kind to you." Lydia smiled.

Linus went to Charlie Brown for advice. "I asked if I should give her a valentine, and she cracked a joke! What should I do?" he asked.

Charlie Brown thought for a moment and said, "If I can't get up the courage to talk to the Little Red-Haired Girl, how am I supposed to help you?"

"You're right, Charlie Brown," Linus agreed. "I have to figure this out on my own."

As Linus turned to leave, Charlie Brown handed him a large envelope covered in hearts.

"Before you go," Charlie Brown asked, "will you give this to the Little Red-Haired Girl for me?"

The next day Lydia showed something to Linus. "Look, I brought a pretty pink ribbon to wrap around my Valentine's Day cards."

Linus thought that meant she wanted him to give her a Valentine's Day card. "Aha!" Linus chuckled. "You *do* want me to make you a valentine!"

Lydia smiled. "Oh, I didn't say it was for your valentine," she told him.

Linus was more confused than ever.

While Linus was struggling to figure out if he should give a valentine to Lydia, one person was not struggling at all: Sally! She had made a big valentine for Linus, and she could not wait to give it to him! Once the glitter on the sparkly heart had finished drying, Sally rushed off to deliver it.

Sally knocked on Linus's door and shouted, "Oh, Sweet Babboo! I made you a pretty, pretty valentine!"

Linus did not answer the door. "I'm *not* your Sweet Babboo!" he yelled from inside.

"Yes, you are!" Sally countered. "It says so right here on this giant glittery heart!" Sally slid the valentine under the door and skipped happily away.

At recess the following day, Linus tried one last time to ask Lydia about Valentine's Day.

While she swung back and forth on the swings, Linus asked, "Do you like poetry? Flowers? Sparkly hearts?"

Lydia was slow to respond. Finally she said, "Girls really like music boxes. And they love when they're gifts from people they care about."

Linus wondered if this was a hint. "So, you would love it if I got you a music box?" he asked.

Lydia kept right on swinging and said, "Oh, I have lots of music boxes!"

Now Linus was really confused.

Linus sighed. "Maybe I should skip Valentine's Day this year and worry about Arbor Day instead," he said.

Moments later Sally found him on the playground. "Hello, my Sweet Babboo. It's me, your Sweet Babbooette!" she cooed. "I made you another valentine."

Linus lost his temper. "I'm not your Sweet Babboo! And I've never even heard of a Babbooette! I don't want your dumb valentine! Leave me alone!" he hollered.

Sally's face, which had been lit up with excitement, suddenly looked very sad. She ran inside, crying. Over on the swings, Lydia scowled. She had seen the whole thing and was angry at Linus for being so mean.

Charlie Brown saw what happened as well. "Linus, what's going on?" he asked.

"I have some thinking, and apologizing, to do," Linus said softly.

Later that day Linus visited Sally. "I'm sorry I hurt your feelings. I liked your valentines very much," Linus said. Then he handed her a card and said, "I made this for you."

"A valentine!" Sally squealed.

"It says 'For My Friend.' Just *friend*, Sally," Linus insisted.

"Friendship can lead to Babboo-ship!" Sally told him.

"Oh, good grief . . . ," Linus whispered.

On Valentine's Day, Linus spoke with Lydia before class. "I'm sorry I haven't been myself lately," he said.

Lydia shrugged. "I hadn't noticed," she lied.

Linus continued carefully. "I just wanted to say . . . Valentine's Day seemed the right time to tell you. . . . Well, I find you fascinating!" he stammered. He handed Lydia a valentine and quickly turned around.

Lydia smiled widely, but Linus couldn't see since he was facing the other way.

Lydia read the valentine and held it close to her. Then she wrapped it in a pink ribbon.

Finally, after what felt like far too long to Linus, Lydia said, "Thank you, Linus. Happy Valentine's Day."

Linus breathed a sigh of relief. "You're most welcome," he said.

"Maybe next year," Lydia said with a nudge, "you can get me a music box!"